ERIC
the Cat with Thumbs!

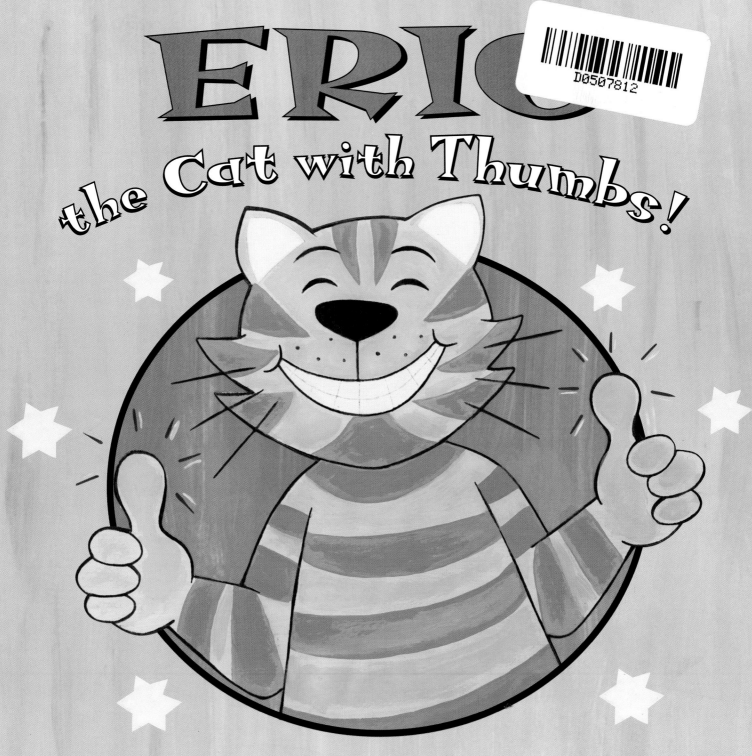

Written by
Louise Rooney

BRIMAX

Illustrated by
Olivia Rayner

Eric was a cat just like every other cat, except in one amazing way. Eric had thumbs!

All the other cats padded about on their dainty paws.

They sniggered at Eric as they chased each other up and down trees.

"Cats don't have thumbs," they mewed together.

Poor Eric was very unhappy.
He couldn't pad about daintily,
as his thumbs got in the way.

He couldn't
climb trees,
as he didn't
have claws.

And he couldn't mew with the other cats;
they just wouldn't let him!

Eric decided to leave his home and find his fortune in the big wide world outside!

TO THE CITY

He WOULD find something he was good at.
He WOULD find a use for his thumbs.
He WOULD show those alley cats!

Before long, he saw a sign that made him quite excited.

Eric marched straight into the cinema and
showed Rupert, the manager, his amazing
thumbs. Rupert was very impressed,
and gave him the job immediately.

Eric set to work. He used his thumbs to take films out of their containers.

He used his thumbs to load films onto the projector.

He used his thumbs to switch on the projector.

But there was one problem. The projection booth was very hot, and cats shed their fur when they get too hot. This is exactly what happened to Eric!

Eric's fur flew everywhere. It got all over the film, and made a terrible mess.

Before long, the actors on the big screen were
so hairy that they looked like monkeys.
The audience hissed and booed,
until Eric felt it was best to leave.

EXIT

Poor Eric, he would have to try something new. He carried on through the city, and before long he came to another sign.

This time, Eric thought, *I cannot fail.*

Eric went inside to apply for the job.
"Those thumbs are just what I need," said Stan,
the pilot. "I'll be doing the flying, and you'll
take charge of the controls," he explained.

Up they went, higher
and higher, and
faster and faster.
But Eric grew
greener and
greener, and
sicker and sicker.

Poor Eric was good at the controls, but he was not good at heights! Stan just about managed to land the helicopter in one piece, and then Eric felt it was best to leave.

FIRE STATION

Soon Eric came to another interesting sign.

This, thought Eric, *is it.*
Into the fire station he went.

The fire chief took one look
at Eric's thumbs and decided
to test him out right there
and then.

He asked Eric to slide
down the pole.

NO PROBLEM.

He asked Eric
to climb up
a ladder.

NO PROBLEM.

Then he asked Eric to spray water all over a little fire. OH DEAR!

The water squirted everywhere, but cats do not like water. Even cats with thumbs DO NOT LIKE WATER!

After the fire was safely put out, Eric felt that it was best he left, and carried on his way.

Poor, poor Eric. He started to think that though his thumbs were useful, he was useless! He was just about to give up and go back home in shame, when he saw one final sign.

Eric decided to have one last try.

Friday night came,
and crowds of curious animals
padded into the theatre. Even the cats
from Eric's alley were there. They all clutched
mysterious invitations to a spectacular show.

They whispered to each other, wondering who the star could possibly be. Then they sat back and waited excitedly for the show to begin.

As the big red curtains swept back, the crowd gasped to see who was on the stage. It was Eric! With one strum of his thumb, he filled the hall with the sounds of a rock and roll tune.

It was the coolest music that the crowd had ever heard, and they cheered and clapped until their paws were sore.

And now, cats all over the world talk about their amazing hero — Eric, the cat with thumbs.

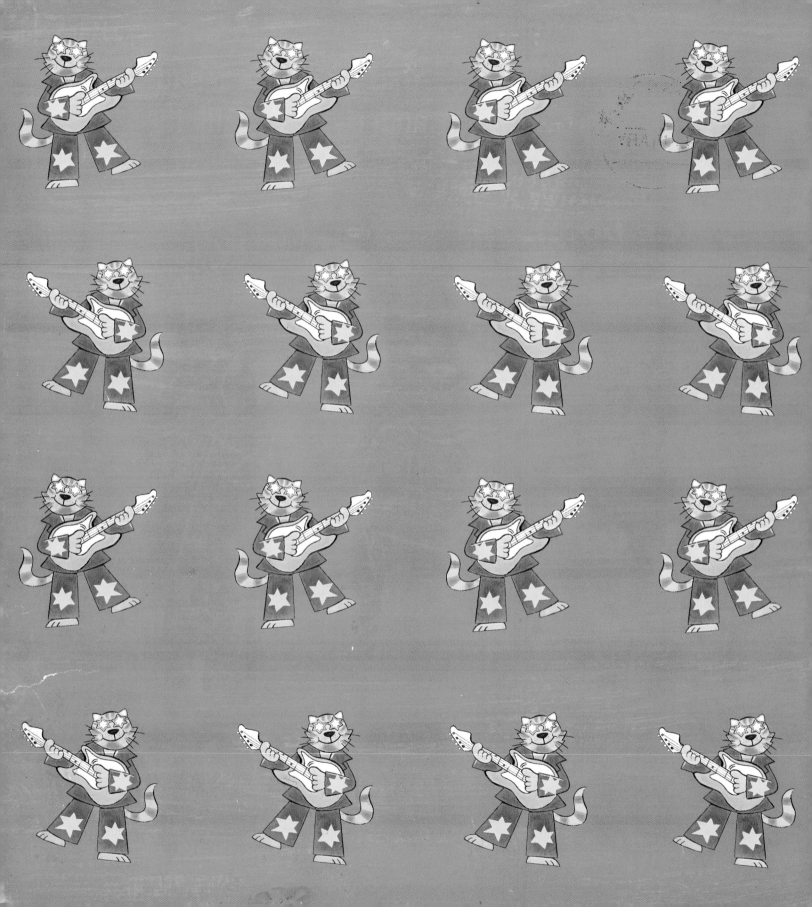